Toys in Space

Some other books by Mini Grey

Traction Man Is Here!
Traction Man Meets Turbo Dog
Traction Man and the Beach Odyssey
Three by the Sea
The Adventures of the Dish and the Spoon
Egg Drop
Ginger Bear
The Very Smart Pea and the Princess-to-Be

For Janet Schulman

THIS IS A BORZOI BOOK PUBLISHED BY ALFRED A. KNOPF

Copyright © 2012 by Mini Grey

All rights reserved. Published in the United States by Alfred A. Knopf, an imprint
of Random House Children's Books, a division of Random House, Inc., New York.
Originally published in Great Britain by Jonathan Cape, an imprint of Random House
Children's Books, a division of the Random House Group Ltd., London, in 2012.

Knopf, Borzoi Books, and the colophon are registered trademarks
of Random House, Inc.

Visit us on the Web! randomhouse.com/kids

Educators and librarians, for a variety of teaching tools,
visit us at RHTeachersLibrarians.com

Library of Congress Cataloging-in-Publication Data is available upon request.

ISBN 978-0-307-97812-7 (trade) — ISBN 978-0-307-97815-8 (lib. bdg.)

MANUFACTURED IN CHINA
May 2013
10 9 8 7 6 5 4 3 2 1

First American Edition

Toys in Space

MINI GREY

Alfred A. Knopf
NEW YORK

That summer night,
for the first time,
the toys were left outside.

The sun went down,

the sky grew dark,

and, for the very first time...

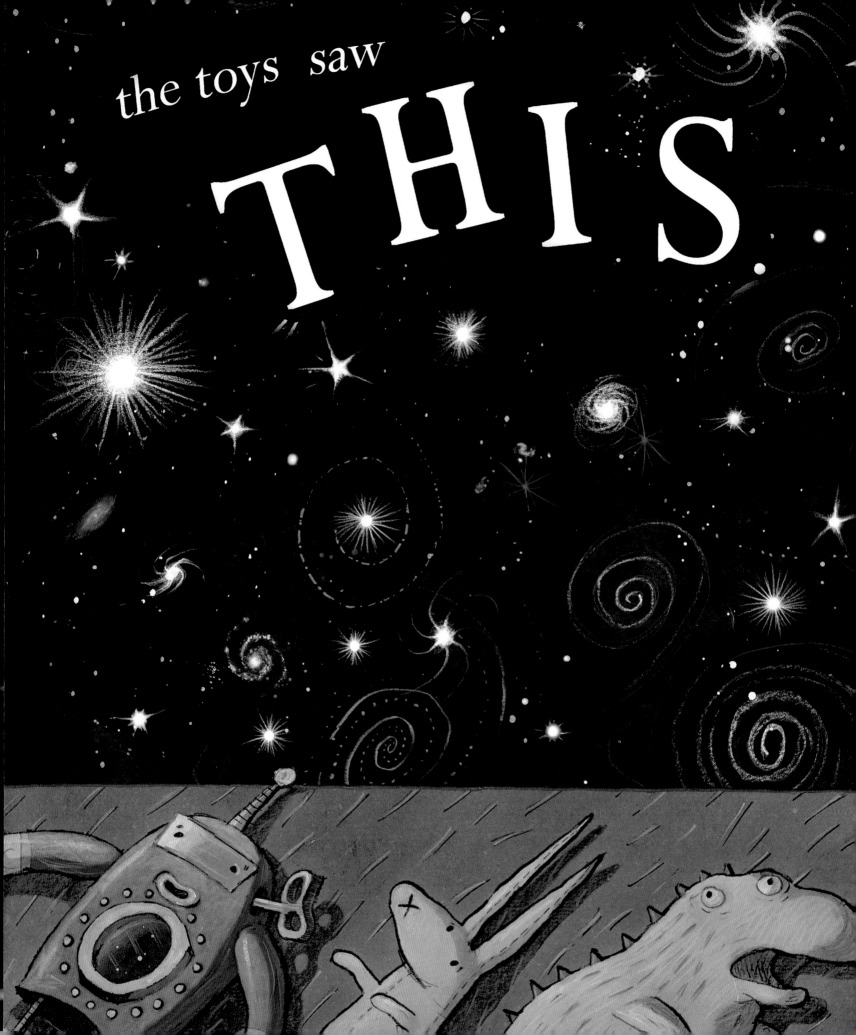

Everyone was quiet
for a while.

"We need someone to tell us a story!" said the Blue Rabbit.

The WonderDoll thought for a moment, and then *she* began.

It was going to be a long night.

Once upon a time *(the WonderDoll said)*,
there were seven toys left out in the garden:

a resourceful Pink Horse,

a brave Small Sheep,

a clever Blue Rabbit,

a strong little Cowboy,

a thoughtful green Dinosaur,

a helpful windup Robot,

and a WonderDoll.

Well, the sun went down and the toys saw the stars for the very first time.

And then one of the stars started to grow. It got bigger and bigger and bigger.

And the toys realized it
was actually not a star at all–
it was a spaceship!

And the spaceship
opened up a bright
hole and
beamed
the toys
up into it.

Well *(went on the WonderDoll)*, the toys were inside the spaceship and feeling a bit worried, as you can imagine.

Then a door opened...

It's a drooling alien! It probably likes to eat pink felt!

It might drool at the toys!

No dang alien is drooling at me!

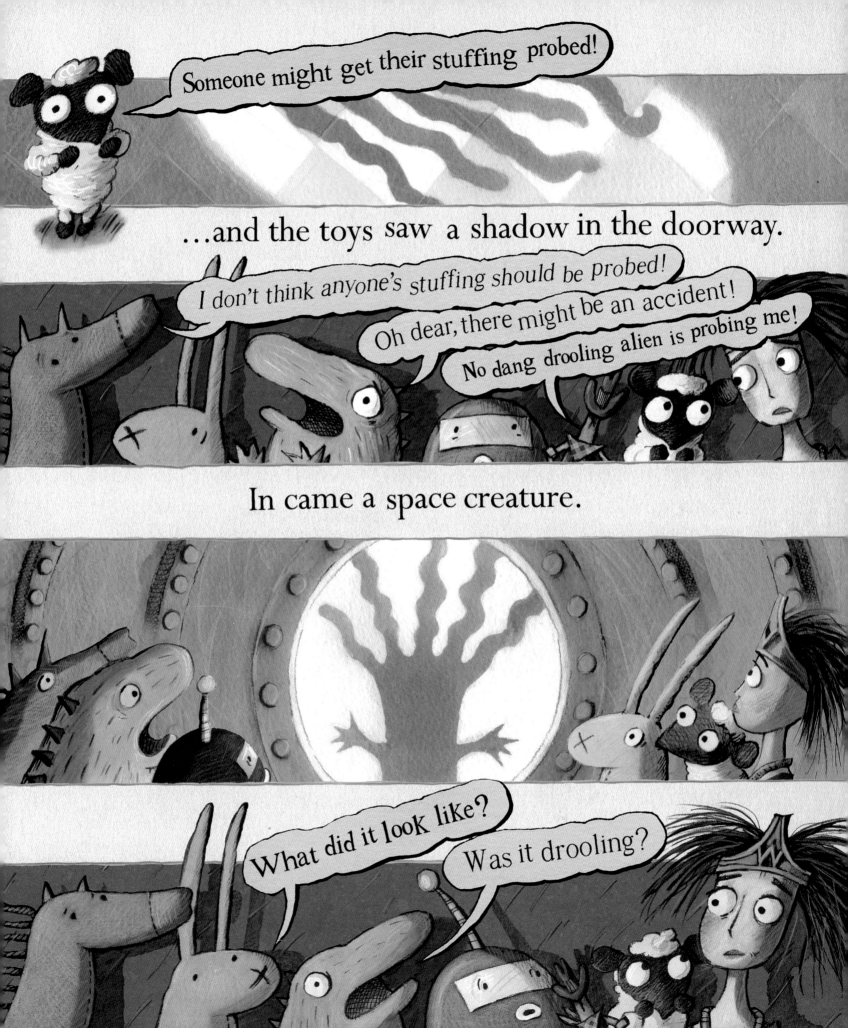

It looked rather like a glove
and it was wearing pajamas
and its eyes were red
from crying.

What was it called?

We will call it the
Hoctopize for now.

The Hoctopize looked carefully at the toys.
But none was the toy it was searching for.

The Hoctopize showed the toys
a picture of its Cuddles, who was
lost.

It took them to the Room of a Thousand Lost Toys.

It had collected them from gardens all over Earth.

SLEEP-O-METER

SLIGHTLY DROWSY

LIGHT SNOOZE

SWEET DREAMS

DEEP SLEEP

SUSPENDED ANIMATION

HEY— You can't just take people's toys without asking!

They all belong to somebody!

They will be missed

The toys helped the Hoctopize to realize that all those Thousand Lost Toys had to be returned to their real homes.

But how do they know where to send them?

Luckily, the Hoctopize was very organized and had labeled them all with their addresses.

It put a stamp on each label to help with the delivery.

Near the Pond
22 Rockery Prospect
Puddlington

Then they parachuted all the Lost Toys down toward Earth.

Picnic Table
Front Lawn
37 Spoon Drift
West Cutlery

Once they had gone, the Hoctopize sat down and cried. It still didn't have its Cuddles.

The toys need to make it feel better!

Then the Dinosaur had an idea—they could have a party to cheer up the Hoctopize.

Everyone had jobs to do:
Blue Rabbit and Pink Horse
made a cake,
WonderDoll
and Small Sheep
made party hats, and
Robot and
Dinosaur did
the decorations.

And what about the Cowboy? What did the Cowboy do?

The Cowboy
organized
all the games.

Hey! You! Stop! You're out!

They played
musical chairs
and musical statues.

It turned out that the Hoctopize was outstandingly good at musical statues,

and won every time.

What was the prize?

Our toys have to return
(*the WonderDoll carried on*).
They each hold a balloon to drift down,
and everybody takes a piece of cake.

The Hoctopize waves goodbye.

And down down down
through dark space
and into blue sky
and through clouds
and toward the ground
float the toys.

The WonderDoll stopped.

The toys opened
their eyes—the dawn
had happened.

It was a new day,
and soon they would
be found.

Oh yes *(said the WonderDoll)*,
of course it will find its Cuddles.

It will be in the last place it looks.

Things
always are.